PIRATE

Blunderbeard

WORST. HOLIDAY. EVER.

Join Pirate Blunderbeard on more adventures:

Pirate Blunderbeard
WORST. PIRATE. EVER.

Pirate Blunderbeard
WORST. HOLIDAY. EVER.

COMING SOON
Pirate Blunderbeard
WORST. MISSION. EVER.

PIRATE
Blunderbeard

WORST. HOLIDAY. EVER.

AMY SPARKES & BEN CORT

HarperCollins *Children's Books*

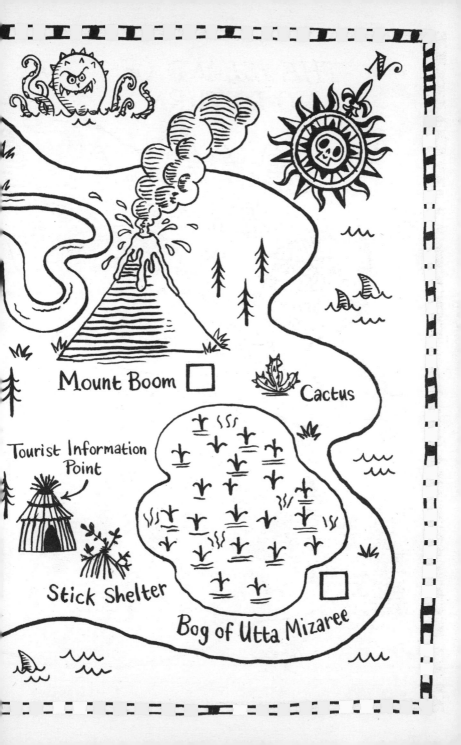

Mount Boom □

Cactus

Tourist Information
Point

Stick Shelter

Bog of Utta Mizaree □

Mum

Blackbeard

Blunderbeard

Hooksy

Pirate Pete

MilDred

Uncle Redbeard

Redruth

Captain Chomp

Barber Rossa

First published in Great Britain by HarperCollins *Children's Books* in 2017
HarperCollins *Children's Books* is a division of HarperCollins*Publishers* Ltd,
HarperCollins *Publishers*,1 London Bridge Street, London, SE1 9GF

The HarperCollins website address is:
www.harpercollins.co.uk

1

ISBN 978–0–00–820185–2

Typeset in Bembo Schoolbook 15pt/26pt
Printed and bound in England by Clays Ltd, St Ives plc

For Abby, who would make a brilliant pirate.
And for my editor, Harriet,
who has made this adventure so much fun.

Amy Sparkes is donating a percentage of her royalties to ICP Support, aiming for every ICP baby to be born safely.

Reg. charity no. 1146449
www.icpsupport.org

SHOCK AS WORST PIRATE EVER WINS PIRATE OF THE YEAR AWARD

TOUGH PIRATE BLACKBEARD ACTUALLY CRIES

LEGENDARY TREASURE FOUND BY CHICKEN??!!

JANUARY 1ˢᵀ

Still can't believe that last year I won the
POTY (Pirate of the Year) Award. Neither
can my big brother Blackbeard. Or Mum.
Or my cousin Redruth. Or my horrible
Uncle Redbeard. Or, come to think of it,
any pirate who's ever met me ...

I owe a lot to Boris. It's not often you come across a chicken who is part-dragon and can sniff out gold a mile away.

I would never have found the treasure hoard in the POTY competition without her. Will be very extra specially nice to her this year.

And that Blaster-Hunter™ invention I made to help find the treasure?

Well, orders are flooding in from lazy, treasure-hunting pirates and my new business, *Blunderbeard's WonderWeird Contraptions*, is up and running. I've put ALL my treasure money into it.

Feeling really positive about my New Year's Resolutions.

1. ~~Stop biting nails.~~ (Except this one. Still too hard.)
2. ~~Employ Blackbeard as my toilet cleaner.~~ (OK, not this one either. PARPS – the Pirates Against Rubbish Piracy Society – fired him as director but then they gave him his job back. Turned out no-one else was as mean as him and they missed him. Humph.)
3. Go on a treasure-hunting expedition with Boris.
4. Make Blunderbeard's WonderWeird Contraptions bigger and better.
5. Get a pet goldfish.
6. Stuff traditional pirating. Be the bestest cupcake-baking, gadget-inventing pirate on the seas EVER.

At last, I am a success! And this year will be the best year I have ever had! ☺ ☺ ☺

JANUARY 2ND

Disaster has struck!!!!

No time to write.

Busy swimming to save my life.

JANUARY 3RD

My life is ruined.

RUINED.

This is what happened — I was working on a brilliant new invention: the Boot-A-Pult™. Pirate boots are so hard to get off — why don't we just wear sandals?! — but the Boot-A-Pult™ just CATAPULTS them off at the end of the day.

Boot-A-Pult™

Step 1: Unfold stick-thing
Step 2: Hook stick-thing into top of elastic band
Step 3: Pull until elastic band reaches pirate's shoulder

Step 4: Release stick-thing
Step 5: Retrieve boot (and stick-thing) from other side of cabin

I was testing the Boot-A-Pult™.

It was brilliant. The boot went flying across the cabin …

And hit Boris! She flapped up into the air and knocked my ladder!

The ladder hit a shelf and my *Captain Cook's Recipe Book* slid off!

The book landed on my clothes-dryer

invention (the ShirtSpinner5000™),

switching it on to TRIPLE SPEED!!

Clothes went flying everywhere …

My Christmas jumper knocked the
lantern off the wall.

The lantern fell down on to my *Extra Extra
Strong Baking Powder for Really Big Cakes* …
which (it turns out) doesn't mix well with fire.

There was a huge

BANG!!!!!!

and then the ship began to sink!

I just had time to grab a few things: Boris, a small bag of emergency gold, my diary, a pen and a clean pair of pants. (Mum says never go anywhere without a clean pair of pants.) Then we swam for our lives!

Luckily, Captain Orlando Hoy (of Lando Hoy Ferries) saw us and picked us up. (For my entire bag of emergency gold …) ☹

Unluckily, the sea was very choppy.

Boris was seasick … all over my clean pair of pants.

Oh. That. CHICKEN!!!!!!

No cupcakes. No ship. No money.

No *Blunderbeard's WonderWeird Contraptions*.

And no clean pants.

My life, as I say, is RUINED. ☹

JANUARY 4TH

Been staying on Mum's ship, the *Golden Squid*, at Dead Man's Cove while I work out what to do.

Blackbeard's there too – his oh-so-wonderful ship is being redecorated.

So I turned up, clutching a half-drowned

chicken and a pair of sick-soaked pants.

He stopped laughing at about teatime.

Used Mum's hairdryer to try to dry
Boris.

Now she looks like this:

Blackbeard started

laughing again.

Hasn't stopped yet.

I want to fire

the Boot-A-Pult™

at his enormous

backside. Shame I

don't have it any more.

Or any of my *Blunderbeard's WonderWeird*
Contraptions. Or any money. Or anything.

Waaaah! ☹

Blackbeard has grown this really stupid, wispy beard. He thinks it's amazing. I think it looks like he's glued some of Mum's cat's fur on to his face. Told him this. Spent the rest of the morning tied to the mast with milk spread on my face and Mum's cat licking me. *Eurgh*.

2pm

Had my revenge on Blackbeard. Got Boris to lay eggs in his hat. He didn't realise and put it on. *Mwahahaha.*

JANUARY 15TH

Blackbeard got his parrot IronClaw to poop on Boris' head. And mine. YUCK. (Wish Blackbeard hadn't fed him squid curry last night.) ☹

JANUARY 23RD

Dropped a crab down Blackbeard's trousers. Just before his mates Hooksy and MilDred came round.

Blackbeard's revenge: they all tied me and Boris upside down to the plank.

MilDred made them take us down, though, after I passed out for the second time.

Painted Blackbeard's new eye patch pink.
He was furious. He shoved Boris in the
cannon to send her flying. He peered
inside to check she was in place …
And Boris burped and set fire to his beard!
I 'helped' by throwing a bucket of dirty
deck-washing water all over Blackbeard.

Unfortunately, Mum came in just then.
She may have got a teensy bit wet too.

Whoops.

She's fed up with us squabbling and says
we have to move out REALLY SOON.

Will be glad to get away from
Blackbeard but where can I go?! ☹

Couldn't un-wedge Boris from the cannon.

Had to fire her out.

She's not speaking to me.

FEBRUARY 10TH

Tried to cheer Boris up by saying she's now beaten the world record for Fastest Chicken Flight Ever. I even offered her those shiny gold buttons she loves.

She's still not speaking to me.

FEBRUARY 20TH

Found burnt holes in all of my pants. Possible that Boris still hasn't *quite* forgiven me.

2pm – Appointment with Captain Cutthroat, Pirate Careers Officer. Port Cutlass.

Without a single doubloon in my squiddy bank, there's no way to restart my *Blunderbeard's Wonder Weird Contraptions* again. So Mum made me get an appointment with the Pirate Careers Officer.

Took a quiz.

This was the result:

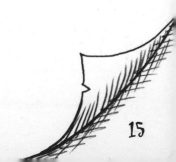

Thank you for using the

Pirates' Information, Direction, Development and Life Enhancement Service

in association with

PARPS

YOUR CAREER SHOULD BE: Jellyfish-catcher. Duties include chasing and catching jellyfish for Jackson's Jelly. Oh, and being stung by lots of horrible, slimy jellyfish.

Great. The only gloves I have are my
Christmas present from Redruth. They're
hot pink. Seriously?! I asked Mum
if she had any kind of
protective headgear
I could borrow.
She came up with
this:

ARGH!

Right, that's it. I NEED to get *Blunderbeard's WonderWeird Contraptions* up and running again!! Somehow!! There's NO WAY I'm catching jellyfish.

10am – Start work at Jackson's Jelly catching jellyfish.

Got fired.

An unfortunate incident with some jellyfish, a rare giant piranha and a can of baked beans. Who knew piranha farts were deadly to jellyfish? It could have happened to anyone. Why does it always happen to me?! And why do people nearby always have cameras??!! ☹

I HATE CAMERAS!

Cameras should be banned. I declare March 13th National No Cameras Day.

The only good news? I lost Redruth's gloves. No-one will ever catch me in them again!

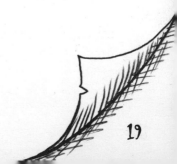

"IDIOT PIRATE
IN PIRANHA DRAMA"

And it gets worse.

Even Deader Man's Cove
The Ocean
March 13th

BARNACLES BLUNDERBEARD!

Have you forgotten that jelly is my favourite
food? I am down to my last fifty packets.
When I next see you, I will string you up by
your toenails, and tickle you with feathers
from your stupid chicken until you are very,
very sick. And **THAT** is if I am in a good mood.

Uncle Redbeard

Ohhhhhhhhhhhhhhhh dear.

Think I'm going to stop opening the
post for a while.

MARCH 18ᵀᴴ

Small mountain of unopened post on my bed.

Back to job-hunting to take my mind off everyone wanting to send me to Davey Jones' Locker.

There are plenty more jobs in the sea. I'm sure my perfect job is waiting just on the horizon.

Right?

MARCH 25ᵀᴴ

Well, so far I have been hired and fired from the following jobs:

1. Gold-Tooth-Polisher at Basher's Gnashers. (Well, I don't think Captain Cutthroat really needed all of his teeth anyway.)

2. Parrot-Groomer, Pirate Pete's Pets. (Why the fuss? Bald parrots look... er... interesting.)

3. Cannon-Fixer, Pirate Claire's Repairs. (I only caused two fires. And who needs walls? Or a roof?)

4. Beard-Cleaner, Barber Rossa's. (OK, so my MuckSucker™ invention shouldn't be used on beards. Now we know. I'm sure Blackbeard will forgive me. Gulp. It's just possible I might be in a teensy-weensy bit of trouble...

MARCH 26TH

Yep.

Pirates Against Rubbish Piracy Society

The Moaning Mariner
Port Cutlass
The Ocean
March 25th

Dear Barnacles Blunderbeard,

As you are well aware, PARPS exists
to make sure that only the finest and
rottenest pirates are allowed to roam
the seas. At our recent meeting, we were

more than slightly miffed to hear that so far this year you have:

Blown up your own ship with *baking powder*. (Couldn't you at least have used a cannon?!)

Used a chicken as a weapon in a series of ridiculous attacks on the Director of PARPS. A *chicken*?!

Really REALLY annoyed Captain Harry Chomp, Senior Officer at SMELLS (Society for Monsters Existing in Large Lakes and Seas, registered charity oooooPS). He wrote a 36-page letter to complain, and I quote:

"My poor kraken is still sneezing after Blunderbeard caused it to have an allergic

reaction during last year's POTY Awards. AND
I still can't unplait its tentacles that got twisted
up, chasing Blunderbeard's stupid chicken! I've
had to tie a ribbon in the tentacles and persuade
the kraken it looks stylish!

Do you know how hard it is to persuade a
snot-dripping, ribbon-wearing kraken it
looks STYLISH?! DO YOU?!"

Single-handedly demolished the entire jellyfish supply for Jackson's Jelly. Just what are we supposed to eat at birthday parties now?! *Again*, I quote from Captain Chomp's letter:

"I am OUTRAGED to hear Blunderbeard has caused damage to a rare giant piranha! I am now looking after an extremely grumpy fish with extremely bad digestion, which has put both of us in a bad mood. Do you know how hard it is to look after a grumpy fish that produces massive farts without warning? DO YOU?!"

and *"If Blunderbeard EVER comes near any of my creatures again, I will personally feed him to the Loch Ness Monster. BOTTOM-FIRST!"*

So you get the idea.

⚔️ Utterly destroyed the magnificent beard of the Director of PARPS, ruining his chance to win the Best Beard Award. (I now have to wear an upside-down tea cosy strapped to my chin, Blunderbeard! NOT HAPPY.)

⚔️ Completely ruined the workshop of Pirate Claire's Repairs. Where are we meant to send our toasters to get fixed?!

⚔️ Made many of the toughest parrots on the Seven Seas go completely bald. They are now refusing to come out of their cages until their feathers have regrown.

We are crosser than Captain Cressida Crosse on the day she sat on that stingray at the annual World's Crossest Pirate Competition (and *that* was scary).
Thanks to you, we will have no jelly to eat at the PARPS and PIDDLES summer party this year, we'll have to eat sandwiches for breakfast and will be forced to wear pigeons on our shoulders. PIGEONS, Blunderbeard.

As you continue to act like a complete shrimp-brain, PARPS are forced to take action (*yet again*). While we consider

your embarrassing and pitiful case and
decide what your fate will be, send
us over a dozen cherry cupcakes with
marshmallows on top. And hope it puts
us in a better mood.

Yours sincerely,

Blasterous Blackbeard

(Director of PARPS)

P.S. I mean it. Watch your step –
or I'll make you trim my toenails!

OK, have just quickly baked a dozen cherry cupcakes with marshmallows on top and sent them to Blackbeard.

I need these cakes to sweeten him up. My fate depends on it.

Please like the cupcakes.

Please like the cupcakes.

Please like the cupcakes.

Wait … there's salt in my sugar jar!!

I must have mixed them up!

But that means …

the cakes …

PARPS …

salt …

I'M GOING TO DIE.

Pirates **A**gainst **R**ubbish **P**iracy **S**ociety

TEMPORARY HEADQUARTERS:

The Moaning Mariner

Port Cutlass

The Ocean

March 28th

Dear Barnacles Blunderbeard,

How can I put this?

33

YOU COMPLETE AND UTTER IDIOT!!!!!!

The twelve meanest pirates on the
Seven Seas have just eaten the
MOST REVOLTING cupcakes in the
history of pirating. What is the matter
with you??!!

Was this some kind of stupid joke?
Captain Slasher the Rather Scary was
very, very sick in Captain Molly McFowl's
hat. Captain Molly threw her hat away,
which hit Captain 'Bones-for-Breakfast'
Hayter in the face. He fell backwards on
to Captain Griselda Gunn. And so it went
on. The fight that followed resulted in:

- Two ripped sails
- One rather large fire
- Eight pirates walking the plank
- One tea-cosy beard thrown overboard
- Four squashed watermelons
- One very big hole in my ship
- A lot of really quite nasty bumps and bruises.

We have had it up to our singed eyebrows with you, Blunderbeard.

Captain Cutthroat (Pirate Careers Officer) has had to go on a very long holiday to try and get used to his new false teeth.

In his absence, PARPS has come up with the perfect job for you.

You (and your ridiculous, gold-sniffing chicken) will be sent on a secret treasure-hunting mission.

More instructions will be given once you arrive. Pack immediately.

JUST GO!!

Captain Hoy from Lando Hoy Ferries will pick you up tomorrow.

Yours sincerely,

Blasterous Blackbeard

(Director of PARPS)

A secret treasure-hunting mission! And they have asked ME! I thought I was going to be in big trouble, but this sounds great! I'm bound to get a share of the treasure and then I can restart my invention business. ☺

I started thinking about what I need to pack. Luckily I made a new Boot-A-Pult™. I might have to do a lot of walking and it'll be useful to take my shoes off at bedtime.

Hmm ... the treasure will surely be guarded by a dragon or something scary. Dragons love treasure. (Just ask Boris.) Will quickly make some dragon repellent to take with me. Mum won't miss her perfume.

DracoRid™ Potion

Ingredients:

Mum's perfume (scares anything away)

Squirty cream (foam can put out fires,

so dragons won't like this)

Tried it out on Boris. After all, she's part-dragon. It works!

She sniffed it, sneezed ten times and her beak swelled up in an allergic reaction. Purple smoke streamed out of her nostrils. She ran out of the door and along the plank as fast as her bandy legs could go. Then she dived off with a triple flip.

(Actually
quite
impressive.
Are there
any Chicken
Olympics?
Maybe I could
set one up and
get rich?)

MARCH 30TH

10am - Packing.

2pm - Give Boris seasickness tablets!!!

3pm - Lando Hoy Ferry coming . . .

Said bye to Blackbeard and Mum. Well, I tried. They were busy having a sword fight at the time, so didn't even listen to me. ☹ All because Blackbeard was showing off a new sword-fighting move and accidentally smashed the picture of Grandpa Greybeard on the mantelpiece. Mum was furious. She was yelling that

Grandpa would have taught Blackbeard a thing or two. He was one of the best pirates ever. Shame he died in that awful storm a few years ago. I'm always up for someone making Blackbeard look stupid. Mum gave me the book Grandpa wrote – *Proper Pirating for Beginners* – for my birthday last year. She said I should take it with me. Might come in handy.

Oh well. Bye, then, everyone.

Don't miss me too much, will you?

Oh, wait. You won't.

The Lando Hoy
ferry arrived
to pick me up
and I climbed
aboard. Captain
Hoy said the
journey would take
a couple of days because the island was
such a LOOOONG way away. He was
also grinning a lot. Something had made
him very happy. He said he had further
instructions to give me when we got closer.
Feeling a teensy bit nervous now ...

APRIL 1ST

CAN'T BELIEVE – PIRATE FERRY –
CAPTAIN HOY HAPPY –
ME STUCK – BIG ISLAND –
BOAT LEFT – BLACKBEARD FAULT –

PANIC!!!

OK, deep breaths. Calm down.

Breathe in.

Breathe out.

PANIC!!!!!!!!!!!!!!!!!!!!!!!!!!!!!!!!!!!!!!!

Breathe in.

Breathe out.

OK. I'm OK now.

That's better.

That wretched Blackbeard!! Just because he's the Director of PARPS, he thinks he can go and do THIS to me. This is the letter Captain Hoy gave me before he chucked me, Boris and my bag over the side and rowed away. No wonder he was grinning.

GRRRR!

Pirates **A**gainst **R**ubbish **P**iracy **S**ociety

TEMPORARY HEADQUARTERS:

The Moaning Mariner

Port Cutlass

The Ocean

March 28th

Dear Barnacles Blunderbeard,

Congratulations on being chosen for the Treasure-Hunting Mission. To the Island of No Return! Bahahaha. The clue's in the name, Blunderbeard. NO. RETURN.

Everyone is so fed up with your disasters that you and your chicken can stay there unless you prove that you're not a complete embarrassment to the word 'pirate'.

Rumour has it that somewhere on the island is a massive treasure hoard, but no-one has ever returned to say for sure. If you can find it, we will come back and pick you up. If not, tough. At least we won't have any more of your ridiculous stunts.

See you later.

Although, probably not.

Yours sincerely,

Blasterous Blackbeard

(Director of PARPS)

P.S. Don't worry. I'll look after all your cupcakes while you're gone BAHAHAHA.

So here I am. Stuck on the Island of No Return.

Looked it up in *Proper Pirating for Beginners*.

OK, this is what it says:

Island of No Return:

This be an island of greatest peril!
Not one doomed soul who set boot on
this island has ever returned! Legend
speaks of a dangerous creature that guards
treasure. ('Course, we don't know where
the legend comes from, because no-one
ever returned to tell it.) Only go to this
island if your very life depends on it.
Death and destruction awaits ye.
YE BE WARNED.

Oh, great. *Now* I feel better.

Captain Hoy chucked us out of the boat and made us swim the last mile. Boris is cross about her (still) damp feathers and refusing to move. Carrying an angry, squawking, soggy chicken on your shoulders is about as much fun as high-fiving an electric eel. Her beak is

still all puffed up from the DracoRid™ trial so she can't smell a thing, let alone the scent of buried gold. Not exactly the best start …

9am - Mum let me bring her old telescope.

Looked through it. Think I can see the Tourist Information Point hut in the distance. Or it might be a big bear in a large hat. This telescope is rubbish.

9.10am - Ouch.

So busy looking through telescope at 'big bear in large hat', failed to notice 'big crab in large rockpool' in front of my foot.

This island hates me. Heading inland, to escape evil crabs.

My toe hurts VERY VERY much. ☹ So now we have to hop all the way to the Tourist Information hut/big bear in large hat. Don't suppose anyone else has EVER hopped round the Island of No Return with a chicken before.

Only me.

This island is huge. Will take me a-g-e-s. Great.

APRIL 8TH

Phew. The Tourist Information Point is not a hat-wearing bear!

All there is to take away is a free treasure map: *Island of No Return Treasure Trail*. It says this:

In your hand this map ye hold;
It leads ye to the secret gold.
Fill in four letters as ye go;
Beware – ye have a deadly foe.
Until, at last, in deepest gloom,
Ye pirate fool will meet your doom.

Oh.
Good.
Grief.

Well, that sounds as cheery as

Blackbeard on bathday. ☹

But what choice do I have??

I NEED this treasure. I NEED to get off this island.

Fair to say, I stand as much chance of survival as a fish in a frying pan. In the desert. On the hottest day of the year.

So here we go.

Wish me luck!

(Gonna need it.)

9am - Still making my way to the first box
on the map.

Made a stick shelter to sleep under last
night.

It worked fine until Boris gave this
almighty sneeze and the whole thing came
crashing down on top of us.

Wish I hadn't tried the DracoRid™
potion on her. Her beak is still puffed up.
Only I could be on a treasure hunt with
a gold-sniffing chicken who has lost her
sense of smell. ☹

And not only does she keep sneezing

my bedroom down, SHE NOW SNORES
LIKE A DRAGON!!!

Wonder if the one guarding the treasure
snores? Hope the DracoRid™ potion
works.

Gulp.

APRIL 22ND

Midnight.

Footsteps.

Someone coming. Woke up Boris to stop
her snoring.

They're coming closer.

Voices.

Male voice: "And when we gets our

hooks on this legendary booty, me hearty, we'll be rolling in gold!"

Female voice: "This is soooo totally cool, Dad. Hey, can I get, like, a new ship? Bigger than Blackbeard's? He's having his all done up at the moment. Thinks he's soooo cool …"

Voices are fading away. They're gone.

Oh no. Oh VERY no. I'm more doomed than the last dodo trying to fly off a cliff on Doomsday.

I know those voices. They strike terror into my very soul. And who are the owners of these dreaded voices?

Uncle Redbeard and Cousin Redruth.

APRIL 23RD

7am

Woke up. Nightmare about being hung upside down and pelted with cannonballs wrapped in pink paper, which then sprouted teeth and ate up all my gold.

Uncle Redbeard and Redruth - here?? They hate me! Uncle said in his letter he was going to string me up by my toenails and tickle me with feathers until I was sick! ☹

I must avoid bumping into the Reds AT ALL COSTS.

My life and my toenails depend on it.

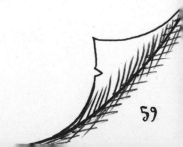

No sign of the Reds. Toenails safe so far.

Arrived at the stinkiest place known
to piratekind. (And that's coming from
someone who's been close to Blackbeard's
underwear drawer.)

It says on the Tourist Information sign:
WELCOME TO THE BOG OF UTTA MIZAREE.
ENJOY A NICE REST WHILE YE SIT SOBBING
AND WISHING YE NEVER CAME
TO THE ISLAND.
TISSUES AVAILABLE IN VENDING MACHINE.
50p.

NO CHANGE GIVEN.

Tissues? Pah. I won't need *them!*
A teensy-weensy bog isn't going to make
ME cry.

Nope. I'm as tough as Mum's seaweed
pancakes. (Yuck, they were awful.)

APRIL 28TH

The bog stretches as far as the eye can see.
It's endless! ☹

Tossed Boris up in the air to get a
bird's-eye view. Probably should have
warned her first. She panicked, crash-landed
on my head and sent me toppling into the
bog. Am now covered in brown slime and
leave a squelchy trail behind me.

Boris 'Puffbeak' doesn't seem bothered at all by this place. Grumph. That's even more annoying.

How dare she be happy?!

Just passed the tissue vending machine. Pah. Don't need them. Won't need them. Don't know what all the fuss is about. This bog is NO problem.

NO. PROBLEM.

This bog smells worse than Blackbeard's socks. ☹

I'll never find the treasure and I'll be stuck on an island with a chicken FOREVER.

There's no point taking another step forward. Waaaaah!

MAY 2ND

Still not taking another step forward.

GO
AND
WALK
THE
PLANK.

MAY 10TH

I hate my stupid life.

I hate the whole stupid Island of No
Stupid Return.

And I even hate my stupid socks.

And, NO, the stupid Bog of Utta Mizaree
is NOT getting to me.

All right??!!

MAY 16TH

Possible that the Bog of Utta Mizaree has
very *slightly* made me a teeny bit annoyed.

Boris still isn't bothered at all – she was

even whistling this morning!

Had a theory: the stench from the Bog of Utta Mizaree is so awful that it makes YOU feel awful. Boris can't smell it because of her puffy beak, so she's fine!

So:

1. Had a good plan: made a 'stick peg', put it on Boris' beak to protect her, then sprayed the DracoRid™ potion everywhere so I can't smell the bog. (It's foul stuff, but still much better than the Bog of Utta Mizaree.)

2. Had a good result: felt better really quickly.

3. Had a bad thought: that'll be most of the DracoRid™ gone, then. Ah. Might not quite have thought that one through.

MAY 20TH

I survived! I reached the end of the Bog of Utta Mizaree! There's a sign:

YE ARE NOW LEAVING
THE BOG OF UTTA MIZAREE.
TURN BACK OR FACE YOUR DOOM!!

Really?? What could possibly be worse than that bog? (Apart from a month-long, foot-washing holiday with Blackbeard.)

Then, just as we were leaving, I saw a strange sight: an odd sock and a pair of grey, faded underpants hanging on a nearby bush. What in the name of Neptune's nasal hair were they doing there?? They're too small for Uncle Redbeard – he's as round as a barrel. And the pants had a big 'A' written on the front. That must be the first letter for the treasure trail.

 Wrote it down in the box on the map. The pants also had the letters 'GG' scrawled on the label. WEIRD. (I know, I know … That's coming from me – the boy hopping round an island with a chicken that's wearing a clothes peg on her beak. Sigh.)

I wonder what is at the end of the trail. I hope it's nice, like 'the treasure'.

And as for this whole *meet-your-doom* thing at the end of the treasure map,

I hope it's not anything ... you know ...
too Blunderbeard-squishing. Yeek.

MAY 30TH

Uh-oh. Speaking of Blunderbeard-
squishing ...

Found a trail of Jackson's Jelly wrappers
on the footpath.

Only Uncle Redbeard eats them like
chocolate bars. (He really should slow down
– after the whole unfortunate piranha-
baked-bean-jellyfish incident, there's not
much Jackson's Jelly left in the world now.)

I need to find the treasure before the
Reds, but I can't get too close to them.

10am
More jelly
wrappers.
This is not
good news.

I *like* my toenails. And it's going to
be so much harder to find the treasure
if I'm hanging upside down from a tree
somewhere. ☹

I really really REALLY must not bump
into them.

Will tiptoe behind, as stealthily and
quietly as a … a … quiet, stealthy thing.

10.07am

Tripped over own feet. Landed bottom-first on a cactus.

May have yelled.

Will work on 'quiet, stealthy thing'.

JUNE 17TH

Jelly-wrapper trail stopped.

That's great! I've lost the Reds!

Hurrah!!!

Oh.

Or Uncle Redbeard's run out of jelly.

Drat.

That means they could be anywhere ...

Yeek!

Actually, make that Double Yeek! (I only save those for special occasions.)

JUNE 30TH

Still following the map. I think I'm getting closer to the second box.

Going to look through Mum's telescope.

AAAARGH!

There's a MASSIVE blinking eye!!! HELP! Some hideous monster is about to eat me and … Hang on …

Moved Boris away from telescope.

Right. Can now see some kind of

mountain ahead. Has anyone in the history of piratekind walked a chicken up a mountain? ☹

JULY 11TH

This island is so huge I'm taking time out to make a WhizzChick™ – the world's first chicken-powered transport. (Note to self: perhaps include in World's First Chicken Olympics?) Can't wait to get *Blunderbeard's WonderWeird Contraptions* up and running again, then I can make a better version. Every pirate will want a chicken just so they can get one of these.

Maybe.

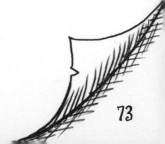

WhizzChick™

Rope harness for chicken (fastened to handlebars)

Storage bag for Chick-O-Snack

Conveyor belt / chain for moving Chick-O-Snack in front of chicken's beak

Gears – to move Chick-O-Snack faster as a reward for faster running

Handlebars

Wooden
board / plank

Wheels / little log
coasters

Works great!

Only fell off 24 times ...

YAY!

Here we are.

WARNING:
YE NOW BE APPROACHING MOUNT BOOM.
THIS LIVE VOLCANO GIVES A SPECIAL FIERY
DISPLAY ABOUT ONCE A CENTURY, 2PM.
REFRESHMENTS AVAILABLE.

Live volcano?! Wonder if this will be the one time in a century that Mount Boom goes off?

Knowing my luck …

Mount Boom is looming ahead of us like a great, big looming thing …

Whoops!!! Explain later!

IN A HURRY!!!!

AUGUST 2ND

Oh. That. CHICKEN!!!

I blame Boris. Boris and her lack of ANY SORT OF SENSE WHATSOEVER.

So yesterday we were on the way to the mountain. The WhizzChick™ was working well.

Everything was fine.

But in my life, nothing is *fine* for long.

Suddenly, the Chick-O-Snack conveyor belt snapped and all the snacks went rolling down the wrong path, to the right of Mount Boom! I tried to call Boris back, but she went mad – flapping, squawking and running after all the escaped snacks!

The path got really rocky and narrow and we were going at great speed!

We rounded a corner and saw a strange-looking box on the rocky wall of the volcano, with pipes everywhere and a great big red button in the middle with an 'E' on it.

'E' for 'Emergency'??!!

FINALLY it clicked in Boris' tiny, TINY brain that she was going to hit the rock. She skidded to a halt. But I was thrown over the handlebars, spun round in the air and hit the big, red button.

With my bum.

Suddenly the red button lit up. There was rumbling … shaking …

'E' for 'Erupt'????

I'll tell you the truth: it is not much fun running away from an erupting volcano with a terrified chicken.

Starting to see why this place is called The Island of No Return. There won't be anything left of you *to* return!!

Note to self: add brakes to WhizzChick™

and make sure the chicken pulling the
vehicle has A BRAIN!!!!

AUGUST 5TH

Lava got stuck in Boris' feathers. Tried to
shampoo it out.

She may have gone pink.

She may be a bit cross.

Written down 'E' in the box on my map.

What do these letters mean and what
do I do once I've collected them?

I wonder where the Reds are? If they
had to shampoo lava out of their hair too,
maybe they are the Pinks now.

Uncle Pinkbeard ...?

AUGUST 20TH

Happy birthday to me ... Well, without the 'happy'.

No birthday cupcake.

No cards.

Not even a rubbish present from Blackbeard.

Spent the day testing Boris' sense of smell. Even tried putting my sock on her beak. She didn't even flinch. (Usually she panics at the smell and runs round in circles for an hour). So she still can't sniff out the treasure for me.

I am NEVER going to find it. ☹ Boo hiss.

Will keep following the map. The next box looks like it's by some kind of river.

Either that, or a very long, thin, blue snake.

Disaster has struck! AGAIN!

We are camping under a coconut tree. I've woken in the middle of the night to find the most terrifying thing next to me: on top of THIS DIARY, a *cannonball wrapped in pink paper!!!*

Note inside.

Hey, Blunders.

What are YOU and your crazy turkey
doing here??!! I went out for a night
walk — Dad reckons the island is
haunted and I wanna see a ghost —
but I found YOU! Did you know you
snore?
I read your diary. Uncle Pinkbeard??!
I took it back to Dad to show him. He
didn't laugh. He looked a bit like Mount
Boom when it went off. (Did you see
that?!)
Dad says he's coming to get you in the
morning.

He was shouting and raging a lot – something about toenails . . .

You are soooo in trouble.

See ya in the morning!

R xxx

I. Am. Dead.

Packed up my stuff overnight and legged it.

Wandering around in the pitch-black with a chicken who has no sense of direction is not the best way to spend the night.

We may have walked headfirst into a tree. (Ouch.) And fallen into a big, smelly pit. (Yuck.)

Sun's coming up now. Can see a bit better. So, how far did we get? We …

Oh no … OH NO … WE ARE STILL AT OUR CAMPSITE!

The tree we walked into? The coconut tree. The hole? The smelly pit that we dug to … do our business.

We've spent the night walking round in circles!

AAAAAAAAAARGH!

Little pink-wrapped cannonballs are flying all around us, left and right!

Quick! To the WhizzChick™!

We're speeding away! Uncle shouting

behind me: "JELLYFISH! PIRANHA!
PINK! BAKED BEANS! BEARD!
IDIOT!" (And something I won't write in
my diary in case Mum ever finds it ...)

Faster, Boris!

B^umpy bⁱt!

Looking behind. Redruth is aiming her
PortaCannon™ and Uncle Redbeard is
waving his sword. (Seriously, those two

really need some stress-management help.)

But ...Yes! We're getting away!

HA! Just blew a big raspberry at Redruth.

She's fired at us!

Whoa!

ARGH! Here comes the cannonball!!!!!!

HELP! We're going to—

AUGUST 31ST

9am

Ow.

Yes, we crashed.

The Reds have tied us to a tree. Am writing with pen in teeth. Sloooooowly.

They have gone back to a Sea Serpent Snack Shack they found along the way because Redruth insisted she wanted some sea-salt popcorn to "watch the show".

Turns out Uncle Redbeard has had time to think.

He's written a whole list of what he's going to do to me! A LIST!!!!

And here it is:

BLUNDERBEARD TO DO LIST

1. Tie up by toenails and tickle with feathers from his stupid chicken until he is very, very sick.

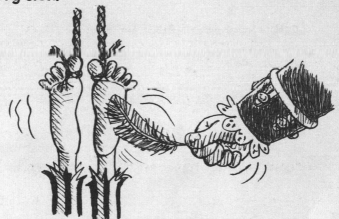

2. Superglue headphones to head and make him listen to Pirate Alberta Screech sing 'Oh, the Woes of the Shipwrecked Rat and his Rather Boring Fleas' OVER and OVER again until he begs for mercy.

3. Put electric eel down his trousers. Twice.

4. Smear strawberry jam from Pegleg's Pantry on his face and release my award-winning collection of Extremely Large and Annoying Ants.

5. Eat very large chocolate cupcake topped with sprinkly bits in front of him and don't let him have a SINGLE crumb! HA!

Uncle Redbeard

Oh. Good. Grief.

This is torture! TORTURE, I tell you!

Not a *single crumb?!*

Trying to persuade Boris to peck through ropes.

Stand more chance of persuading Blackbeard to brush his teeth.

For the love of cupcakes, Boris, JUST PECK!

She pecked my nose.

Oh. That. CHICKEN!!!

3pm

Yes!! Finally free. Only because I told Boris a roast dinner would be on the menu if she didn't hurry up.

More later.

Running to save my life, my ears and my toenails.

SEPTEMBER 1ˢᵀ

So … the Damage Report:

WhizzChick™ is utterly ruined.

My bum really hurts.

And my favourite trousers have

got a BIG hole in them.

This is all Redruth's fault. I should never have invented the stupid PortaCannon™ for that cruel, heartless girl. (Although I'm actually really pleased with how well it works. Yay.)

The Reds are going to be even MORE furious now that I've escaped. I wonder if they or the Island are going to finish me off first?!

SEPTEMBER 8TH

Still ahead of the Reds.

But they could catch up any time, with their LIST and their popcorn!

Boris' beak is looking a little de-puffed.

Maybe, just maybe, she can sniff out the gold now. Will let her try.

It could be a brilliant short cut to the treasure!! And that means escape from the island and the Reds!

Hurrah! The end is in sight! ☺

SEPTEMBER 12TH

Or not. ☹

We've been wandering around following Boris' nose.

So far she's found an old boot, a comb and a cactus shaped exactly like my hat.

I. Give. Up.

SEPTEMBER 20TH

9.30am

Decided it's better to follow the map rather
than a crazy chicken. There's another box
to fill in by the river so we're walking
alongside the water now.

Having to drag Boris along. I haven't
got time for this. We need to keep ahead of
the Reds! But Boris has gone crazy! It's as
if she's scared of the water. Or something
in the water.

She's probably scared of something
really silly, like a stone … her reflection …
or a teeny-tiny fish …

There's absolutely not something

completely and utterly EVIL hiding in the river, which has completely and utterly freaked her out because we're completely and utterly going to die.

Right?

11.00am

There's a little line of boats moored up in the river.

And a sign:

REEKY RIVER RIDES
Requires 1 x token
Relax down the river
and don't look back,
me hearties!

Good. Fine.

Found a box of
free tokens. All the
tokens have the
letter 'V' on the
back. That must
be the next letter.

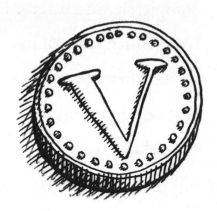

Written it down in the box on my map,
whatever *that* means.

Just need to get Boris on the boat now.

12pm

Boris is a little reluctant to board.

Currently hiding up a tree.

No problem. I can handle this.

2.00pm

Oh. That. CHICKEN!

3.30pm

STUPID ... CHICKEN ... GET ... ON ...
THE ... BLASTED ... BOAT!!!!!!!!!!!!!!!!!!!!!!
!!!!!!!!!!!!!!!!!!!!!!!!!!!

4.30pm

Have a black eye and possibly a broken
finger. Boris has pecked a HUGE hole in
my trousers.

But finally on the boat.

Wasted so much time with that
ridiculous bird!!

At least the Reds aren't—

Hang on.

Looking through Mum's telescope.

That's either a two-headed dragon in a dressing gown running at alarming speed ...

OR ...

ARGH! THE REDS!! THEY'RE COMING!!!

Token in! Boat engine starting!

Phew. We're getting away. We're saved!

4.50pm

AARGHHHHH!

Life hates me!

Explain later!!

SEPTEMBER 21ST

10am

Well, yesterday was interesting!

The boat ride had only been going for a few minutes when Boris suddenly started squawking like someone had eaten her last Chick-O-Snack. All her feathers were sticking up on end!

I peered over the edge of the boat and finally saw why.

A completely and utterly evil SHARK! Teeth and pointy bits everywhere!

What kind of stupid shark lives in a river??!

A hungry one!

Just when it couldn't get any worse, the bottom fell *out* of the boat … it just opened up underneath us! Me and Boris fell *into* the river and went underwater! Good grief, that shark needs to say hello to a toothbrush. Instead it said hello to Boris' tail and my leg!

Luckily, Boris only lost two feathers but the shark ripped off half my trousers! At this rate I'll have no trousers left!!

We just made it on to the riverbank in time.

AMAZING how quickly a chicken can swim when it wants to!

This island is DEFINITELY trying to finish us off. But WHO or WHAT wants to get rid of us?

12pm

Catching breath. Lost sight of Reds.

At huge, dark, gloomy wood. Why can't these places ever be sunny and happy and filled with cake shops?

I hate PARPS for dumping me on this island.

Tourist Information sign reads:

WELCOME
TO THE WOOD OF WORM AND WOE

Pah. *Welcome?!* As welcome as a piranha in your pants.

Looking through telescope.

Uh-oh.

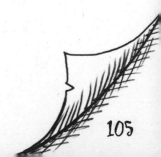

Two-headed dragon in dressing gown coming closer. Can feel my toenails twitching.

Boris doesn't like the look of the wood either. Trying to hide under my hat.

The wood looks like a good place to hide from the Reds. Maybe the treasure is buried in here.

And worms …? How bad can it be?

PLEASE DO NOT FEED THE WORMS.
THEY BITE.

Bite???!!

Boris hiding in my T-shirt.

SEPTEMBER 25TH

Am walking round and round in circles
and keep getting lost!! The wood is
massive! At least that will help me hide
from the Reds. I wonder if they're in here
somewhere too?

No sign of worms yet. We're perfectly safe.

SEPTEMBER 25TH

This is a worm.
This IS OH
VERY
VERY
BAD.

OCTOBER 2ND

Sssshh. Hiding from worms.

OCTOBER 4TH

Turns out the worms don't like the
DracoRid™. Ha! Take that, stupid worms!
I know no fear!

OCTOBER 6TH

Run out of last drops of DracoRid™.
  Sssshh. Hiding from worms.

OCTOBER 13TH

I have a plan! The Exterm-A-Worm™!
  Also have a chicken.
  She doesn't know about the plan …

Exterm-A-Worm™

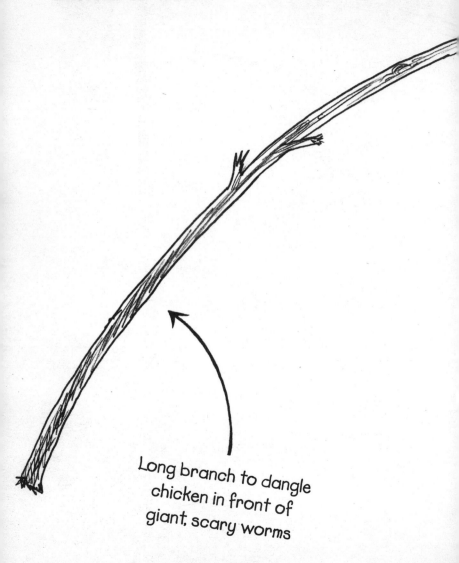

Long branch to dangle chicken in front of giant, scary worms

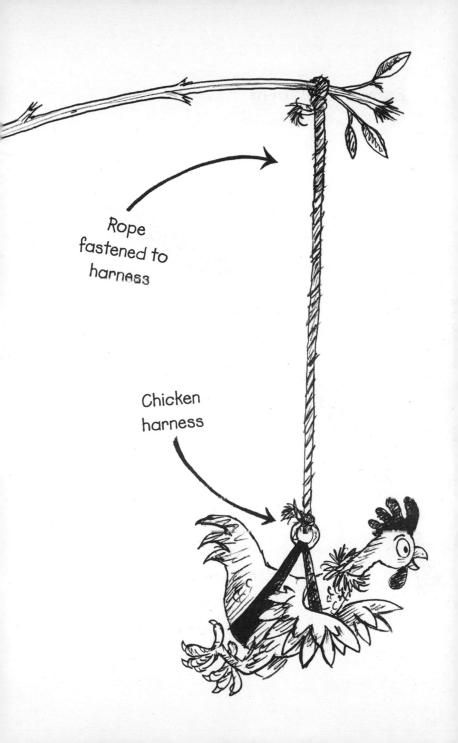

Rope
fastened to
harness

Chicken
harness

OCTOBER 16TH

7.00am

All ready to put my cunning
Exterm-A-Worm™ plan into action.

Just need to persuade Boris to get into
the harness. Won't take a minute.

7.00pm!!!

Boris in harness! FINALLY!

Turned out she wasn't entirely happy
about the worms. I thought chickens were
supposed to *eat* worms. OK, these worms
are tall as a mast, wide as a barrel and
have teeth the size of daggers. But she's just
being fussy!

Well, she's in. So *now* I'm all ready to put my cunning Exterm-A-Worm™ plan into action.

Wish us luck. We're going in.

Death or glory!!!!

7.02pm

… Or hiding up a big tree.

Neptune's nasal hair!! Those worms have big teeth!!

I fear this is the end. Unless my Exterm-A-Worm™ works, we shall be overcome and gobbled by worms. A dreadful and woeful fate for a brave pirate and a magnificent (if slightly ridiculous) chicken. Farewell, cruel world. Farewell.

OCTOBER 20TH

HA!!! We live!

I was magnificent, swinging the
Exterm-A-Worm™ left and right! Up
and down! Round and round! The worms
couldn't move quickly enough! And in the
end, Boris actually enjoyed it! She was
squawking and flapping. She even got
a bite out of the biggest worm (which I
have named WormKing). Of course, that
was after its tail slapped me round the
face and tore off my other trouser leg.
The remains of my trousers are hanging
on to me by a thread!

But the point is: WE WON!

And now the worms all look
like this:

There was a letter carved on the tree
by WormKing.
    'C'.

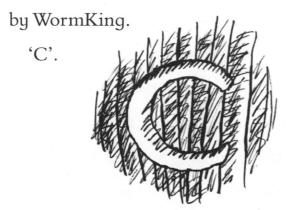

Written it in my map box.

Anyway, it is highly likely that I'm the cleverest pirate to have braved the worms, armed only with a chicken.

Hmm. Also highly likely that I'm the *only* pirate to have braved the worms armed only with a chicken. Really need to get a decent sword ...

Speaking of swords ... still no sign of the Reds. Have I finally lost them??

OCTOBER 26TH

Made it to the other side of the wood. Catching our breath.

Had a thought – if I ever set up the Chicken Olympics, we should have

worm-taming. Boris is bound to win. Then
if I don't find this treasure, at least I might
be a rich and famous worm-tamer.

On a deserted, freaky island.

All by myself.

Forever. ☹

OCTOBER 27TH

OH,
WHERE
IS THAT
TREASURE??

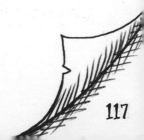

OCTOBER 28TH

I've got to think of a plan! What do I do
now? What kind of rotten treasure hunt
IS this? I've got all the letters – why are
there no more clues?

Oh.

Wait.

Clues …????

YES! OF COURSE! The letters!

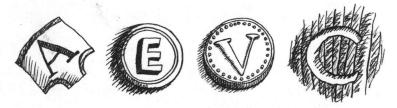

They must be the only clues I need. But
what do I do with them? What does it mean?

OCTOBER 29TH

10am

The letters must stand for something.

An

Enormously

Vast

Codfish!

So, the treasure is inside ... a big ... fish ...

Hmm, maybe not.

An

Extremely

Vile

Cockroach!!

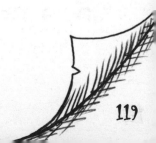

Yeek!! I hope not. Had enough of cockroaches when Blackbeard put them in my muffin mix that time. Can't believe I thought they were crunchy raisins. Grrrr.

This is hopeless.

10am

ARGHHHH!

Incoming cannonball.

Wrapped in RED. Cousin Redruth must be REEEEEEEALLY mad.

Note inside.

Blunders,

Oh, man, are you in trouble. We got
in that Reeky Ride boat to follow you.
The boat's bottom fell out. Then Dad's
bottom fell out! The shark got some
tasty rump. You must have heard Dad's
wailing. My ears are still ringing. He
is now in an even WORSE mood and is
soooooooooo going to feed you to
whatever dreadful monster is guarding
the treasure, wherever it is.

Laters. Well — sooners. The end of
the wood is just in sight and then we'll
catch up with you and your stupid turkey.

R.

P.S. No kisses. Your fault my ears hurt.

12pm

Need to think! Need to THINK! I must figure this out quickly!

Have ripped some pages out of my diary and written down the letters on each page. Maybe that will help.

ARGH! Boris has run off with 'C'!

OH. THAT. CHICKEN!!

12.10pm

Rugby-tackled Boris to the ground.

'C' flew out of her beak.

Now she's mucked up all the letters! She's pecking at the 'C'.

Wait.

Bit longer …

SHE'S A GENIUS! (And very bad at playing rugby.)

It's not what the letters stand for at all – it's an anagram! All the letters need to be muddled up to make a new word!

Now she's pecking at the 'C'! I need to make a word starting with 'C'.

CVEA

CEVA

CVAE

12.12pm

CAVE!!!!!!!!!!!!!!

The treasure must be in a CAVE!

Oops, probably shouldn't have shouted that out loud.

12.13pm

Pink cannonball.

Hey Blunders,

Thanks. We heard that. Don't bother racing us. We're soooo going to find the cave first.

R xxx

12.15pm

Keep calm. I'll find the treasure first.
I'll be fine.

12.16pm
PANIC!!!!!!

They're going to find the treasure first! All is lost!

12.17pm

OK ... Think!! Think! We need a cave. Best place to try is by the sea!

Heading to the sea NOW!

12.20pm

Wrong way!!

Heading to the sea ... NOW!

OCTOBER 31ST

7am

Boris sniffed! Proper sniffing! Not like her sniff with an upturned beak when I take off my boots, but a proper "I-can-smell-gold" sniff! And her beak is finally looking better.

Ladies and gentlemen, we're back in business!

10am

I can see the sea!

And Boris' bum. I really should insist on being the leader.

WELCOME TO THE HAUNTED CAVE.
ENTER AT YOUR OWN RISK.
NO FLASH PHOTOGRAPHY.
TREASURE TRAIL ENDS HERE.
WELL, THIS BE THE LAST THING YE'LL EVER DO . . .

Haunted?!

That ... doesn't ... sound ... good ...

And ... just a thought ... the treasure trail ends here?

So someone wants us to find the cave.

Someone wants us to go in.

Knowing how friendly this island is? That ... doesn't ... sound ... good ... either ...

The cave can't really be haunted.

There's no such thing as ghosts.

Nope. I'm not scared at all.

AT. ALL.

OK, I've changed my mind!! Forget
the treasure. I'd rather swallow a jellyfish
whole than go inside.

PARPS will never rescue me now. I shall return to the Wood of Worm And Woe and take the crown from WormKing.

I am destined to spend the rest of my life as the king of a bunch of giant, grumpy worms.

Alas! This is, regrettably, the end ...

WHAT???!!
BORIS!!!!!!!!!!!!!!!!!!!

Oh. That. CHICKEN!!

She's gone berserk! She must have got a waft of gold! She sniffed, drooled, did a triple somersault in the air – *Note to self: Chicken*

Olympics? – and darted off into the cave!!

The ***Haunted*** Cave!!!

Full of ghosts that can't be really there at all because ghosts absolutely completely probably don't exist.

Do they???

Oh, help.

Well, what can I do? I can't just leave her.

Though maybe she likes it in there. Probably lots of gold ...

Is there gold?

Just peered inside cave. It's pitch-black. Can't see any gold. Can't actually see anything.

I'd better go after her. She IS my chicken.

OK, can't put it off any longer. I suppose

I'll rescue her. Although maybe first I
should just—

ARGH! Pink cannonballs! Shouting!

The Reds have caught up!

OK, OK!! Wish me luck! Got no choice!

I'M
GOING
IN!!!

I write this diary to record the last known
movements and thoughts of the brave
Barnacles Blunderbeard, on his heroic
quest to rescue his chicken from the
notorious, deadly Haunted Cave on the
perilous *Island of No Return*.

2pm

I have been forced into Haunted Cave
due to fierce ambush by big, scary pirates
known as the Reds. As I entered the cave,
two huge torches inside suddenly lit up.

Made me jump but at least I can see to write of my brave and heroic last deeds. (As I sit on the floor hiding behind a very large rock.)

2.04pm

Cannonballs have stopped. The Reds have entered the cave, muttering things like, "idiot boy", "baked beans". I assume they are talking about someone else they met on the island. Ahem.

2.06pm

Have decided to be really brave and tiptoe a little way behind the Reds in the hope of finding and rescuing the poor, helpless and extremely stupid chicken. Also, in the hope that if we are attacked by a ghost, they'll pick on the Reds first and give me time to escape. Gulp.

2.08pm
Sshhh. Still tiptoeing behind the Reds. They have no idea I am here.

2.09pm
ARGH! What's that? A vampire bat?! Argh, it's coming back! Youch! Tripped backwards over rock. That's the remains of my trousers gone! Oh no! Yuck! I've been plopped on by a vampire bat! Oh, wait ... It's not a bat. It's ... Oh! I hate pigeons!!!

Great. Now the Reds have heard me.
And I am going to die wearing only
my pants and dripping with pigeon poo.
Farewell, cruel world.

2.10pm

THEY'VE GOT ME!

HELP!

    Uncle tried to stuff a jelly wrapper up my nose. Got out of his deadly grip – then fell over a stretched-out rope on the cave floor.

2.11pm

Eerie, ghostly wails echoing round the

cave. Chains rattling! The end is upon us!
Wish Boris was here.

2.12pm
What's that?! A grey, ghostly figure!
The Grey Ghost! (Will call it GG for
short!) Strange lights are flickering on the
cave walls! Uncle Redbeard has run off
down a tunnel. (Wimp!) Redruth standing
her ground. Maybe she's not so bad. She's
loading up the PortaCannon™. Here we
go!!! Wonder if it works on ghosts ... Argh!

2.13pm
Apparently not!
Running!

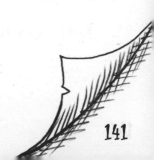

2.15pm

We've gone down a tunnel. Wow!! Found
a chamber FULL of treasure! Crowns!
Jewels! Coins! And ... Uncle Redbeard!
He's stuffing his bag full of gold!

Argh! Ghost coming down tunnel! What
should we do? We're all trapped!

2.16pm

Redruth hurls goblet. Misses the ghost.

Scares the pigeons. Am wearing more poo.

2.18pm

A laugh … an *evil, throaty laugh!* Grey

Ghost – GG – so close. Reaching out its

arm!

It's over.

Nothing can save us now!

2.19pm

Hang on … Do ghosts have throats?

2.20pm

Can they laugh?

2.21pm

Squawking? *FLAPPING?!*

2.22pm

BORIS!!!

2.23pm

She's flapping above the Grey Ghost! She's
squawked and dropped an egg on
the GG's head! The throaty laughing's
stopped!

2.24pm

The GG just said, "Arrrr. Them.
PIGEONS!"

Can ghosts talk???

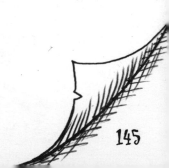

145

2.25pm

Boris flapping wildly around cave!

GG flapping wildly after Boris! She's really

getting the hang of that triple somersault.

Uncle screeching at Boris – he's snatched

a sword from the treasure pile! Oh no,

you don't, Uncle – LEAVE MY CRAZY

CHICKEN ALONE!

Need something to throw! Something to ...
AHA!!!! Quickly pulled the Boot-A-Pult™
foldable stick out of my bag. Attached
to my shoe.

Aim ... fire!

PEOWWWWW!

Look at it fly! Knocked the sword right out of his hand. HA! TAKE THAT, YOU BIG BULLY! A CRASH! Boris has flown into the wall! She's hit a *light switch!* I can see everything now! Wires and cables all over the cave! The eerie music has stopped! It was coming from a speaker on the wall! Boris has saved us! The Grey Ghost looks like a person in a costume, flying with wires! I need to get a photo of all this!

2.26pm

GG roaring: "Me sign says 'NO FLASH PHOTOGRAPHY'! I hates cameras! Why be there always CAMERAS! I declares today be NATIONAL NO-CAMERAS DAY!"

2.27pm

Weird – I said that too (sort of). The GG is going mad! Shouting about cameras and pigeons! He's thrown off the costume! Hurled it at Boris! Boris has crashed into the wall! She's knocked out! And the Grey Ghost … the GG … It's … It's Grandpa Greybeard! But he's … *dead?!* Then he must REALLY … be … a … ghost …

Uncle Redbeard screaming and
pointing at Grandpa. Grandpa's thrown a
goblet in the air – it's landed on his head!

He's fallen on top of me … can't move …
can't breathe … Ooh, head gone all fuzzy-
buzzy. Can't think ~~proberly~~ ~~propally~~ very
well. Grandpa? Greybeard? GG? Grandpa
… Ghostbeard …? Not exactly completely
dead, then … All going black … Farewell …

6pm

Well, that was interesting.

Luckily it was not my destiny to be squidged to death by a red-bearded, barrel-bellied bully. Not today, anyway.

Turns out Redruth was not impressed with her dad – she rolled Uncle Redbeard off me and shoved him in a corner. She says a frozen fish finger has more guts than him.

She saved my life.

Drat. That means I owe her one. And I *bet* she won't let me forget it …

I woke up to find Grandpa Greybeard prodding me with a golden walking stick.

"Ah, Barnabus!" he barked.

"Barnacles," I said quietly.

"Where in the name of Davey Jones be yer trousers, boy?"

"Er …" Not sure I wanted to explain that.

"And why be you on this here island?"

"Er …" Or that.

"On yer feet, boy!"

I stood up and placed my hat over the front of my pants. "Er, Grandpa? Not being rude, but you're meant to be dead. The great storm?!"

Grandpa grinned. His teeth were so black. It's like he had dominoes in his mouth.

"Dead? *Dead?* What be the point in that? 'Course I not be dead! But I be rich.

When me ship was wrecked in that storm, I swam me ashore. Landed by this here cave and found a mighty shiny welcome! I ain't having no rotten pirates getting their hooks on me treasure. And a booby-trapped island makes sure of that! HA HA HARRRRR!"

"So *you* rigged the volcano and the Reeky Rides boats …" said Redruth behind me.

Yeek! Had forgotten she was around too. Quickly moved my hat to cover the back of my pants.

"And I bet you did the treasure clues in

case anyone survived! So you could finish them off here," she said.

"And YOU'RE the dreadful monster?" I said.

"Aye and aye again!" roared Grandpa. "And the Bog! Did ye like me Bog?"

I remember the greying underpants. GG! Written inside the pants! "Grandpa," I said, not sure I wanted to know the answer, "were they *your* pants at the Bog?"

Grandpa jiggled around happily like an octopus with an itchy bum. "Aye! I washes me grimy underwear in that bog. It will stink forever! Haharrrrr!"

(Hmm … it's just possible that being alone on the island for several years has

made Grandpa a little bit woo-woo.)

"Well," said Grandpa, "ye didn't give

up at me bog, ye didn't get blown up by

me volcano, ye didn't get gobbled up by Colin—"

"Colin?" asked Redruth.

"Me shark. Soppy old fish."

Soppy old fish?!

"Ticklish spot under the chin. And me worms didn't get ye and ye survived me Haunted Cave! Ye be the only ones who has! That's put me in a generous mood, that has." Then he picked up a treasure chest and gave it to Redruth. "Ye got guts, girl," he said and winked. Then he picked up a smaller treasure chest and came to me. TO ME!!!! I was going to get the treasure! PARPS could come and get me! I was saved!!

"And ye ..." Grandpa twisted his grey moustache from side to side and frowned. I brought my hat back to cover the front of my pants and held my head high. "And ye ...Well, ye got an *interesting* chicken." He shoved the treasure chest in to my hands. Dropped my hat. Fell over on to my bum. Well, it was heavy! (Not complaining!) I had the treasure! I could get PARPS to come and rescue me!

I WAS SAVED!!!!!

"Aye!" Grandpa continued. "That be one strange chicken. Got a bit of a beak for treasure."

Suddenly a mountain of gold started moving. Boris appeared, a crown perched

wonkily on her head and a medallion
dangling from her completely depuffed
beak. She looked at me and squawked
before diving back into the gold.

"Oh, good," I said. "She's definitely back to normal!"

"Normal?" Redruth said, rolling her eyes.

Grandpa raised a bushy eyebrow. "Ye thinks that's a normal chicken … Hmm. And they thinks *I* be crazy. Anyways!" he roared, dragging me to my feet. "I feels a change in the wind!" He swaggered over to where Uncle Redbeard was now cowering in the corner, terrified. "What say, me hearties, we leaves this useless pile of pigeon plop to guard me treasure while we feels the swell of the seas in our bellies?"

"I can come aboard your ship?" I said

in delight. "Then I don't need PARPS to come and rescue me after all!"

"PARPS? What ye be meddling with PARPS for?" said Grandpa, spinning round to face me. He squinted his little black eyes.

"Oh … er … long story." Thought we'd save that for another day. Hopefully one that never comes.

"Hmm," Grandpa growled, then (phew!) he turned back to Uncle Redbeard.

"YOU!" he bellowed in his face. "Stay here or the Grey Ghost will be back to get ye! Whoooooooo! Haharrr!"

Uncle Redbeard whimpered and nodded.

Grandpa grabbed some sacks of gold

and then turned to us. "I'll teach ye both about being a proper pirate! To me ship! Last one there be a rotten squid!

HAHAAAAAAAAAAARRRRRRRR!"

He pulled a piece of rope dangling from the ceiling and disappeared through a trapdoor in the cave floor!

Redruth and I looked at each other and shrugged. Redruth staggered forward with her treasure chest and jumped after Grandpa.

I called a protesting Boris from the gold and then, holding my treasure chest tightly, we jumped through the trapdoor!

Suddenly we
were whizzing
down this
twisty-turny
chute until
THUMP!
We landed on
the deck of
Grandpa's ship!
The finest ship
I'd ever seen!
(Way better than
Blackbeard's.
Smug grin.)

"Right, me hearties!" Grandpa said, and peered at me. (I tried to look all tough and piratey. Hard to do when you are standing in your pants, covered in pigeon poo and have a chicken perched on your shoulder.) "Afore we sails the Seven Seas in search of danger, death and the perfect fish-finger sandwich, let's go and pay a visit to your mother! Hahahahaarrrrr!"

And so the ship began to move.

The Breath O'Death

Just off the Island of No Return

The Ocean

November 1st

Dear PARPS,

Thank you so much for your kind
offer of rescuing me from the Island of
No Return after you cruelly dumped
me there. However, I am writing to
let you know that I no longer need
your help. I have (with the help of my
incredibly brilliant, talented chicken)
survived the Island of No Return.

I am, in fact, returning as I speak …
well, write … well, scrawl. (Sea's a bit
choppy.)

I am aboard the fearful ship, the
Breath O'Death, run by the even
more fearful pirate, Grandpa Grumpus
Greybeard. I have got oodles of lovely
treasure in my chest and I'm going
to use it to restart my *Blunderbeard's
WonderWeird Contraptions* business,
instead of giving it to you.

Yours, (blowing a big raspberry),

Pirate
Blunderbeard

Inventor, Senior Tester, Chief Executive, Baker
Blunderbeard's WonderWeird Contraptions

Christmas on Mum's ship with Blackbeard,
Redruth and Grandpa. Mum gave me a
new telescope. Blackbeard gave me his
pink eyepatch. Grandpa gave me his new
book that he'd been writing on the island:
Proper Pirating for Beginners: Volume 2. And I
couldn't believe what Redruth gave me for
Christmas: a pet goldfish!! Humph! When
she nicked my diary, she must have read it
from the *very beginning* – that was the only
New Year's Resolution yet to be sorted!!!

Perhaps she is just being nice? Or is she
saying she knows all my secrets, because
she's read my diary? Hmm.

(Note to self: keep an eye on Redruth.
And on possible Spy-Fish. And buy
padlock for diary.)

Grandpa said if I sail with him, he'll
let me use his ship to restart *Blunderbeard's
WonderWeird Contraptions!* He's generous …
if a little scary at times.

Just one thing left to do before we set
sail …

9am

Called Blackbeard on to the *Breath O'Death* to say goodbye. He can't believe Grandpa is taking me and not him.

As Blackbeard stood by the plank, I released my Boot-A-Pult™. Hit him on the backside. Such a beautiful dive. Even Redruth laughed.

9.10am

We have set sail!

Just time to write some New Year's Resolutions. (Though I'm not sure they are a good idea. I always end up in trouble with this list.)

Anyway …

1. Stop biting nails – THIS YEAR I WILL DO THIS.

2. Teach Boris how to be a homing chicken (she could take postcards to my brother Blackbeard – he'll be so jealous. Haha).

3. Get Blunderbeard's WonderWeird Contraptions well and truly going again!

4. Find out what Redruth (and her Spy-Fish) are up to…

5. Survive an adventure with Redruth and Grandpa Greybeard. I hope.

New Year's Resolutions:

1. Teach the lily-livered kids a thing or two about pirating!

2. Face death and danger on the Seven Seas (and be back in time for me evening rum)!

3. Risk life and limb and settle me business with THE BOSS once and for all.

"Shiver me windpipes, Barnabus!
Picked up wrong diary.
Haharrrrr!"

!!!!! Who's 'The Boss'? And exactly whose life and limb is Grandpa going to risk? Gulp. Next year is going to be an interesting year.

Don't miss Pirate Blunderbeard and Boris's first adventure . . .

And if they survive the Island of No Return join Blunderbeard and Boris on the Worst. Mission. Ever . . .

WORST. MISSION. EVER.

Sailing the seven seas with Grandpa Greybeard sounded like a fun holiday, even though we DID have to take my annoying cousin Redruth. But it turns out that Grandpa has a secret plan to capture the ship of Dread Pirate Dreadlocks – winner of the *Pirate Monthly's* Scariest Pirate Award. Easy peasy pants.

What could possibly go wrong...?

Pirate Blunderbeard